Anna's Adventure

Written by: Bernardene Van Epps
Illustrated by: Susan Parker

To order additional copies of this book, contact:
Xlibris
1-888-795-4274
www.Xlibris.com
Orders@Xlibris.com

Dedication

I would like to dedicate this book to:
   Professor Donna Davenport, who encouraged me to write.
   Susan Parker for bringing Anna alive with her Ilustrations.
   And my Mom, Jeannette, who is my best critic and best friend.

Anna woke up so excited because she was going on a special hiking trip. She was going to climb the great skeleton that stood in the back of her classroom. You see. Anna stood about one inch in height and could not see or touch the skeleton like the other students in her class. Since she was very strong and knew how to climb like a mountain climber, she asked her teacher, Miss Carr, if she could climb the skeleton and discover for herself how many bones were in the human body. She was told that there were 206 bones of the human skeleton and she wanted to find them. After packing her gear and eating a good breakfast, Anna set off.

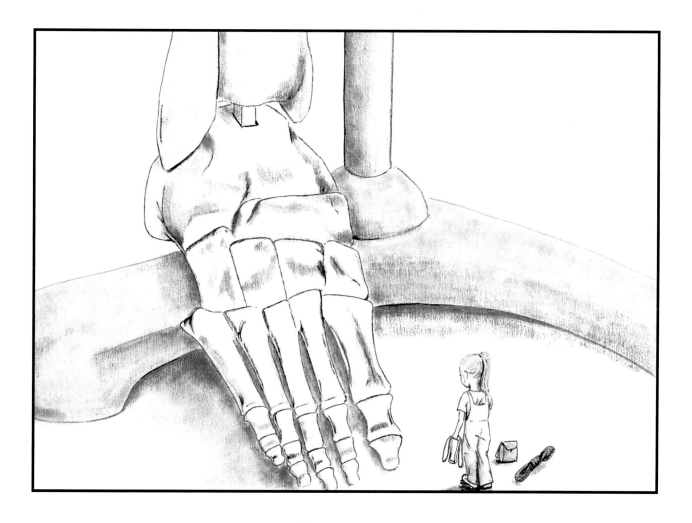

Anna started at the right foot of the skeleton and counted 14 phalanges (toe bones) with the big toe only having 2 bones. Next were the 5 metatarsals and then the 7 tarsal bones; 3 cuneiform, 1 cuboid, 1 navicular, 1 talus, and 1 calcaneus (heel bone).

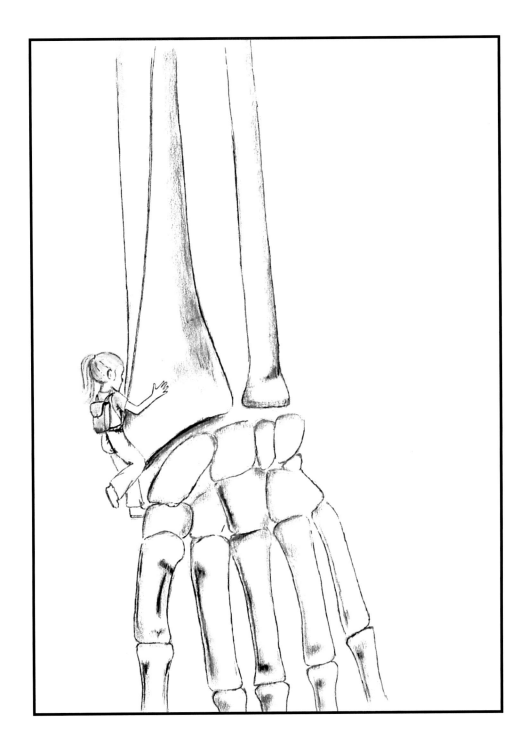

Anna had to get her climbing gear out so she could start climbing the leg of the skeleton. She decided to climb up the tibia since it was bigger and she could just view the fibula from the tibia. But before she climbed too high, she wanted to check out the "ankle bones", the medial malleolus of the tibia and the lateral malleolus of the fibula. This was amusing to Anna that the "ankle bones" were from two different bones instead of one bone.

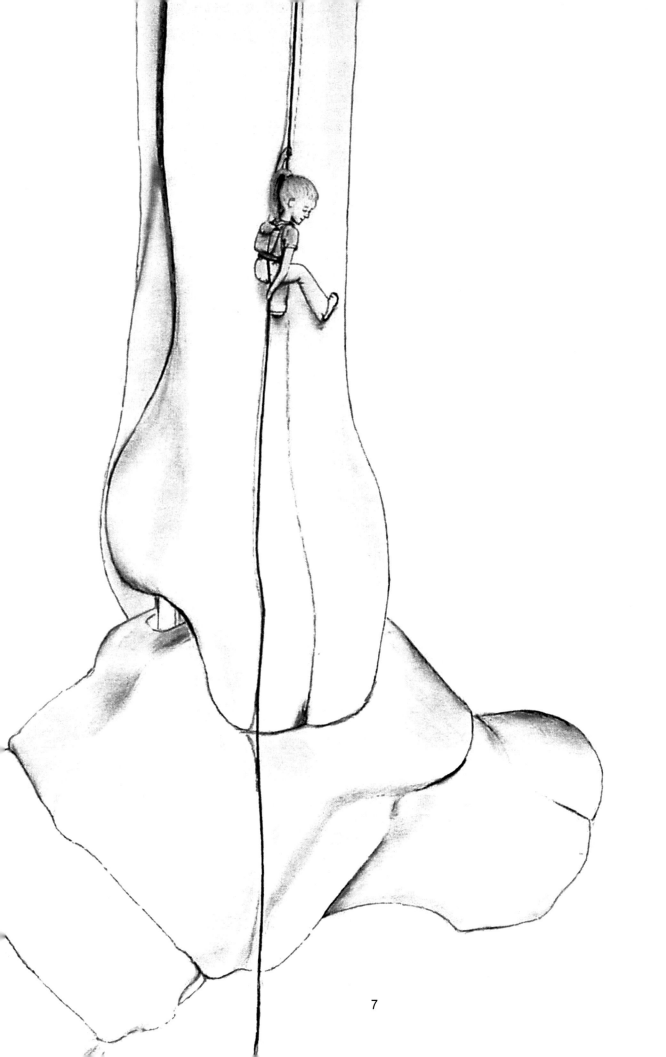

As Anna was getting closer to the proximal end (toward the core of body) of the tibia she could see a bump protruding towards the and anterior (front) of the skeleton. As she got closer to this bump, she realized it was the patella (knee cap). When she got to the patella, she could see that is was located at the base of the femur, the largest and heaviest bone in the human body. She continued up the shaft of the femur and found the greater trochanter (a part of the bone Anna could feel on the lateral side of her leg) and the lesser trochanter on the medial side of the femor. Anna decided to take a rest at the neck of the femur and observe how the head of the femur fits in the acetabulurn (hip socket) of the coxal bone (the pelvis).

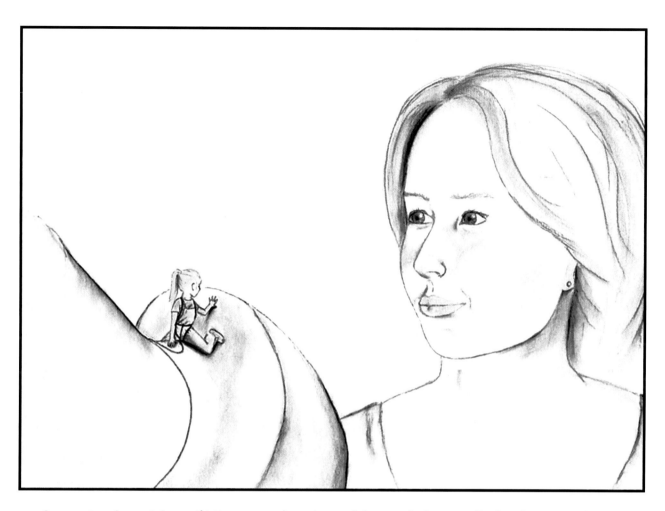

Anna took out her little note book and jotted down all the bones she saw:

14 phalanges

5 metatarsals

7 tarsals

1 tibia

1 fibula

1 patella

I femur

---

30 x 2 (for two legs) = 60 bones

"Are you alright, Anna?" Miss Carr asked.

"Yes, Miss Carr. I'm doing just fine, thank you. I'm just taking a rest before I continue on," she replied.

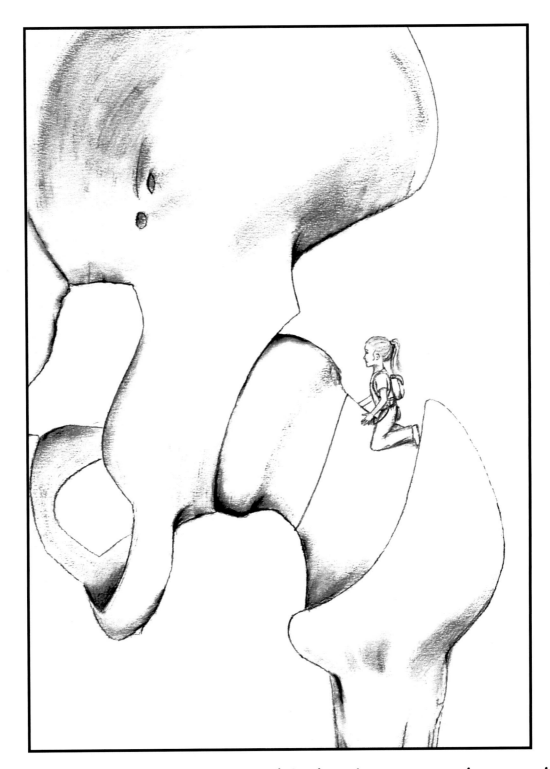

After a few more minutes, Anna picked up her gear and proceeded to the coxal bones. She stood in amazement at seeing the fused bones of the ilium, which was so big to her; the ischium, the part of the bone she could feel when she sat on something hard; and the pubis, located in the front. She hooked up her climbing gear and crossed the iliac crest to get to the sacrum.

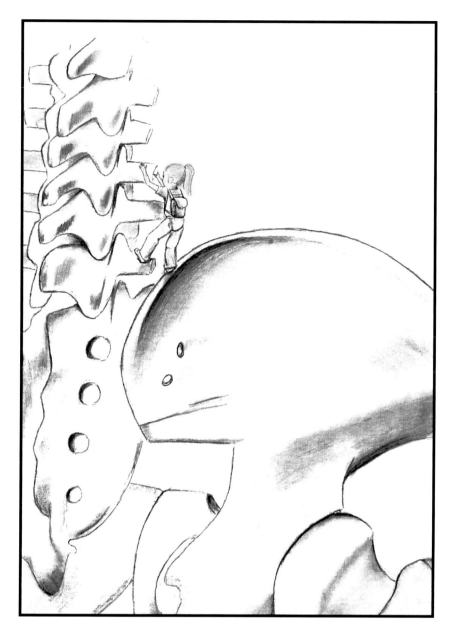

When Anna got to the sacrum, she could not believe it was part of the vertebral column because its vertebrae were fused together. She noticed the coccyx bone (tail bone) was fused as well. Now Anna was ready to climb to the top of the vertebral column. She found the 5 lumbar vertebrae were big and she could see why they needed to be for they had to carry a great deal of weight. Next came the 12 thoracic vertebrae that articulated with the ribs. From this view she could see the 7 pairs of "true ribs" that also articulated with the sternum, the 3 pair of "false ribs" that connected in the front by cartilage, and the 2 pair of "floating ribs" that did not connect to the front at all.

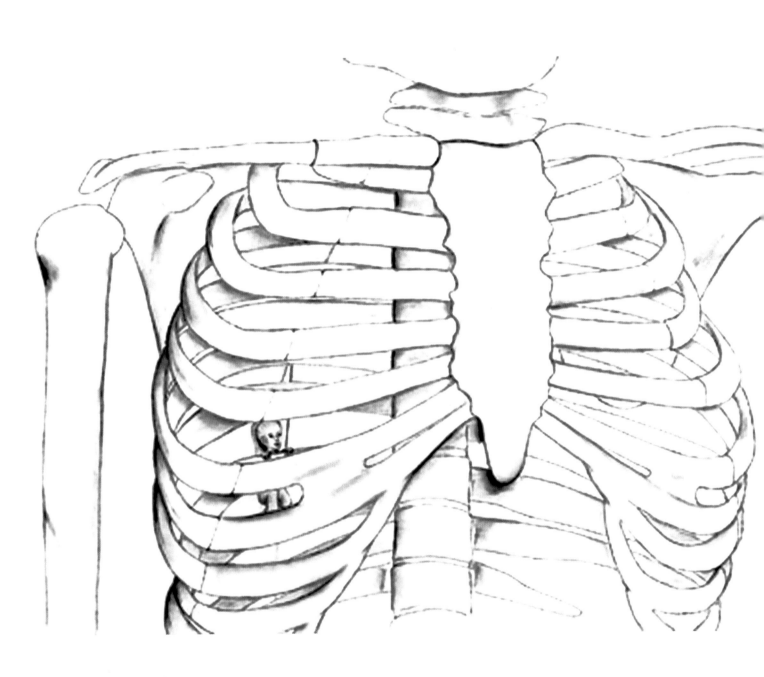

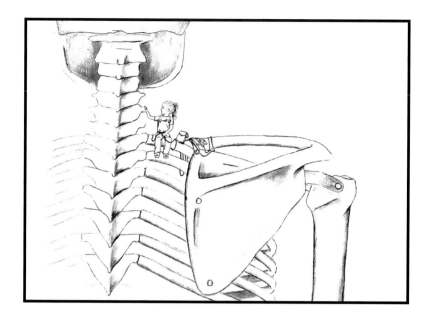

Before Anna continued to climb to the cervical vertebrae, she examined the sternum and observed the xiphoid process located at the bottom (inferior) of the body of the sternum and the top (superior) of the body was the manubrium. Then it dawned on Anna that before she continued on to the skull, she needed to see the arm bones. Anna knew she had to walk on the clavicle (collar bone) to get to the humerus (upper arm bone), but first she had to walk on the first rib from the T—I vertebra to get to the clavicle. Anna's stomach was telling her that it was lunch time so she sat on the first rib, took out her lunch and ate it while observing the 7 cervical vertebrae. Anna noticed a bone protruding from the front of the cervical vertebrae and could not remember what it was.

She called to her teacher, "Miss Carr, what is this bone that is sticking out in front of the cervical vertebrae?"

"Well, Anna, that is the hyoid. It is a bone that does not articulate with any other bone," Miss Carr replied.

"Oh, yes, I remember you mentioning something about this bone. Thank you, Miss Carr."

Anna took out her notebook to tally up all the bones she had seen so far:

2 coxal bones

1 coccyx

1 sacrum

5 lumbar

12 thoracic

1 sternum

14 "true ribs"

6 "false ribs"

4 "floating ribs"

7 cervical

1 hyoid

_____

54 plus 60 = 114

So far Anna counted 114 bones.

It was time to pack up and continue her journey. On to the clavicle!

After climbing onto the clavicle, Anna walked toward the shoulder and saw that the clavicle was connected to the scapula (shoulder blade). She looked to where the humerus connected to the scapula and found the glenoid cavity (shoulder socket).

Anna took out her climbing gear and proceeded down the arm so she could count the bones. First, was the humerus, what a funny name for a bone but it helped her to remember it. When she came to the elbow she could see where the radius (lateral) and the ulna (medial) joined the humerus. Anna decided to climb down the radius and observe the ulna just like she did with the tibia and fibula of the lower leg. As she was descending down the shaft of the radius she could see the shaft of the ulna. Once she came to the distal (furthest away from core of body) part of the radius, Anna could see the head and the medial styloid process of the ulna. What was confusing to Anna was that the ulna's head was distal from the core of the body while all other arm and leg bone's heads were proximal to the core. If that was the only thing confusing her, then Anna thought she was doing just fine.

Now Anna was ready to check out the wrist and hand bones. She was at the articulate facet of the radius connected to the scaphoid and lunate, two of the four proximal carpal bones. The other two she saw were the triquetrum and the pisiform. The other four distal carpals were the hamate, capitate, trapezoid, and the trapezium. That made a total of eight carpals. She then moved down to see the five metacarpals and the fourteen phalanges (finger bones). There was the thumb with only two phalanges just like the big toe. Well it was time to head on up to the clavicle again and then to the skull.

Once Anna got to the clavicle, she decided to observe the seven cervical vertebrae a little more. In order for her to check out the two top vertebra, the axis and atlas, she had to climb inside the base of the skull. So up she went. To get to the top of the axis, Anna had to crawl through the atlas which is superior to the axis. Here she could get a better understanding of how the skull moved.

The last part of the great skeleton that Anna had to look at was the skull (cranial), but before she did that she decided to add up all the bones she had seen so far.

1 clavicle

1 scapula

1 humerus

1 radius

1 ulna

8 carpals

5 metacarpals

14 phalanges (fingers)

_____

32 x 2 (arms) = 64

So the 114 bones from her last count plus what she just added came to 178 bones.

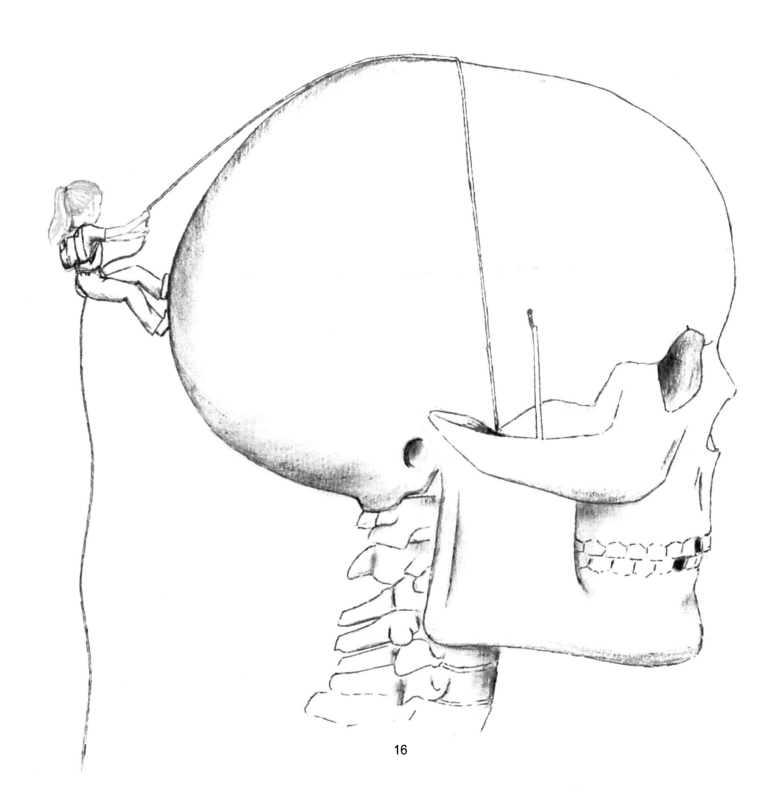

Anna had to decide how she was going to observe the skull. She finally decided to go to the occipital first, which is on the posterior or back part of the skull, then work her way over and around. After climbing over the occipital, Anna worked her way to the top of the skull so she could put her right foot on the right parietal bone and her left foot on the left parietal bone. At this point Anna felt like a great mountain climber, but was missing her flag to stake her claim of accomplishing this amazing task of climbing a human skeleton. (Not too many people could stake that claim Anna thought.) Anna regressed for she had more to accomplish. She lowered herself down to the right side of the skull to take a look at the temporal bone, then moved more toward the front to see the sphenoid. Anna remembered Miss Carr telling the class that the sphenoid alone looked like a butterfly and was the only bone that goes horizontally through the skull.

Anna had to go around the zygomatic bone, one of the facial bones, in order to find the next cranial bone, the ethmoid which she saw inside the orbit (eye socket). She decided to check out the other facial bones before she headed up to the last cranial bone, the frontal.

While standing on the maxilla (just below the nose), Anna could see the lacrimal located anterior to the ethmoid. She then worked her way to the nasal bone and looked down into the nasal cavity. There she could see the vomer, located right in the center of the cavity, and on the sides she saw two inferior nasal concha. Anna dropped her rope so she could swing down to the mandible (jaw bone) and check out the skeleton's teeth. This skeleton had some teeth missing.

Now it was time for Anna to head up to the top by way of the frontal bone.

So off she went. By the time she got to the top, something was bothering her. She had a feeling that she was missing some facial bones. She called to Miss Carr and told her about all the bones she had seen and knew that there were fourteen facial bones but came up with only twelve.

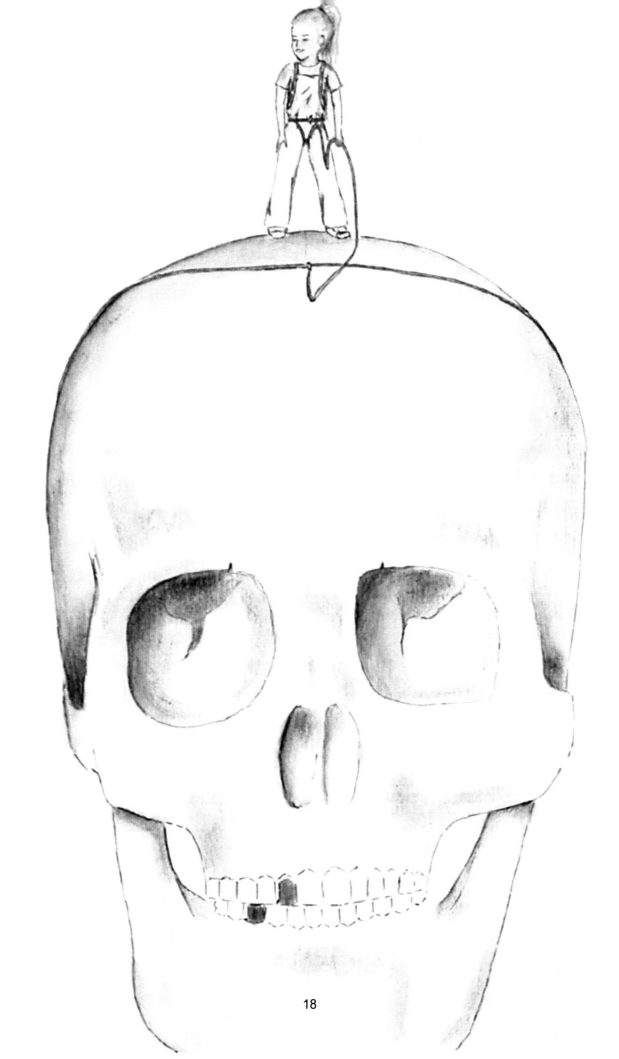

"Did you happen to see the two fused palatine bones, Anna?" Miss Carr asked.

That was it! Anna missed the palatine bones. Miss Carr explained that the palatine bones were located at the roof of the mouth. Now Anna had a count of fourteen facial bones.

Anna was very tired and decided to take a long, well deserved nap. But before she went to sleep she took out her notebook to add to her list of bones.

Cranial bones
1 frontal
2 parietal
2 temporal
1 occipital
1 sphenoid
1 ethmoid
_____
8 cranial bones

Facial bones
2 nasal
2 maxillary
2 zygomatic
1 mandible
2 lacrimal
2 palatine
2 inferior nasal concha
1 vomer
_____
14 facial bones

So Anna's total of bones came to 200. What happened to the last six bone and where were they? Anna was too tired to think so she closed her book, spread a blanket out and lay down. After her nap she would ask Miss Carr about the six bones that were missing from her list.

CAN YOU GUESS WHAT THE SIX BONES ARE AND WHERE THEY ARE LOCATED? (HINT: THE SIX BONES ARE IN THE SKULL)

ANSWER:

2 malleus, 2 incus, 2 stapes = 6 bones in the ears.

3 in each ear.

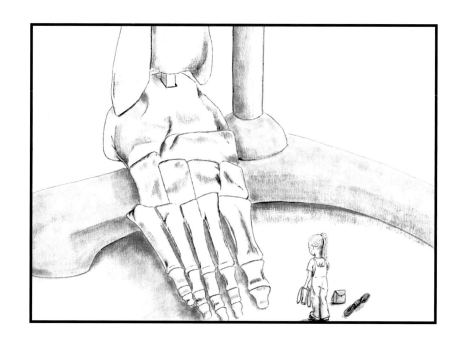

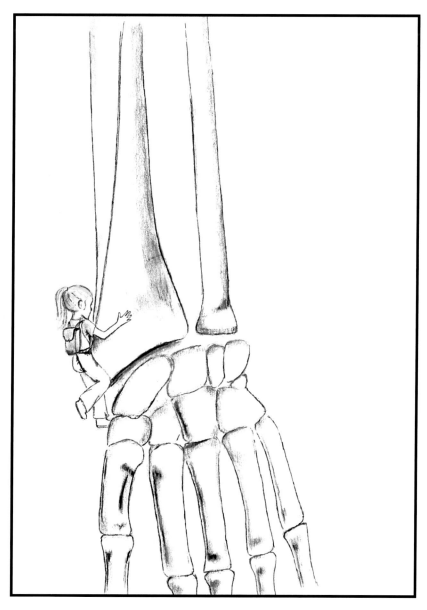

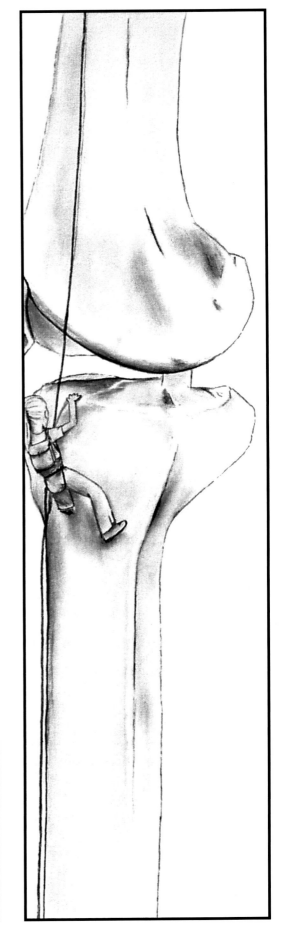

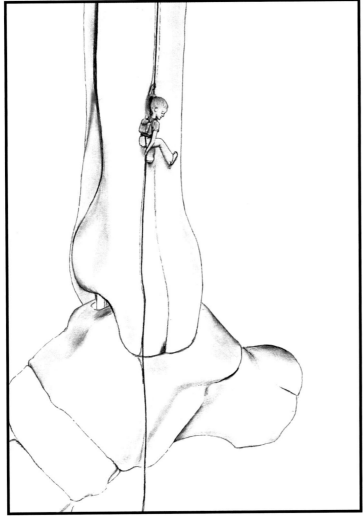

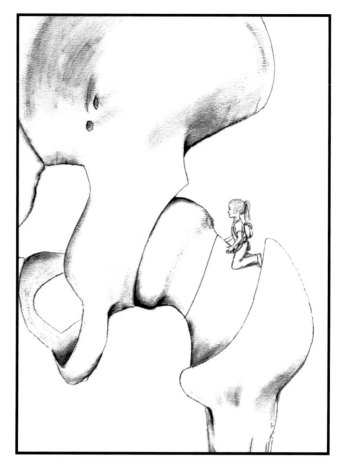

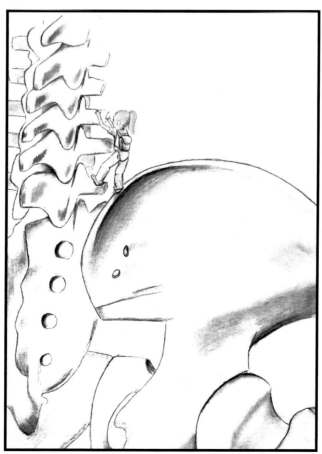

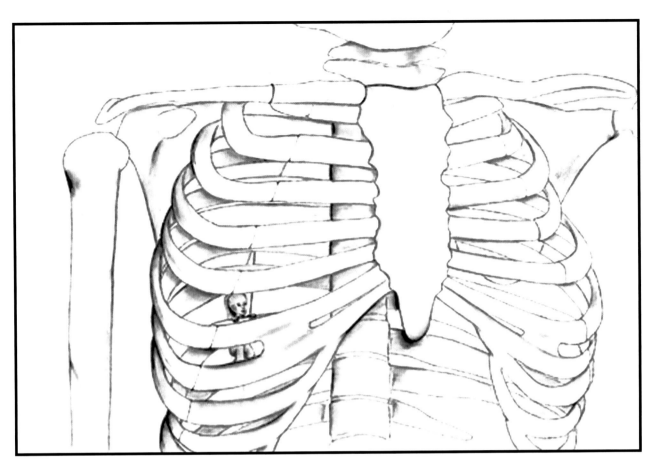

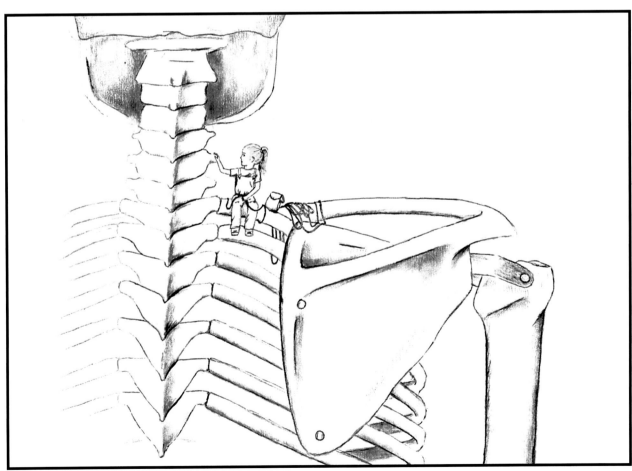

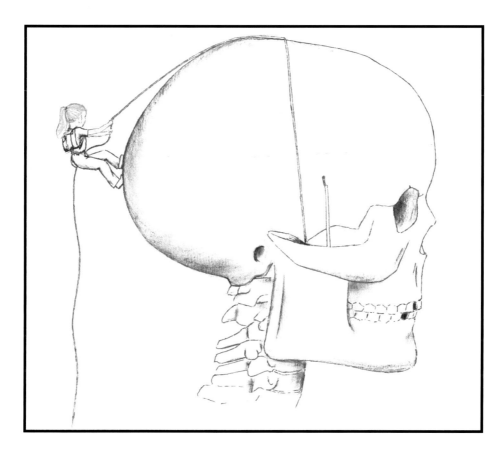

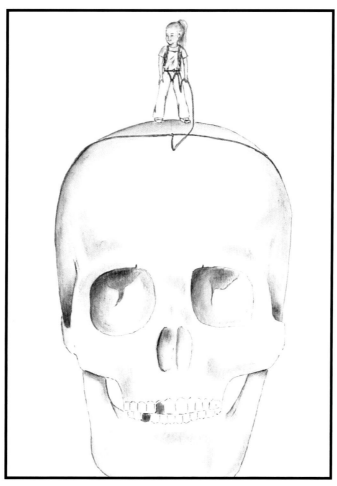

Printed in the United States
By Bookmasters